R0174949463

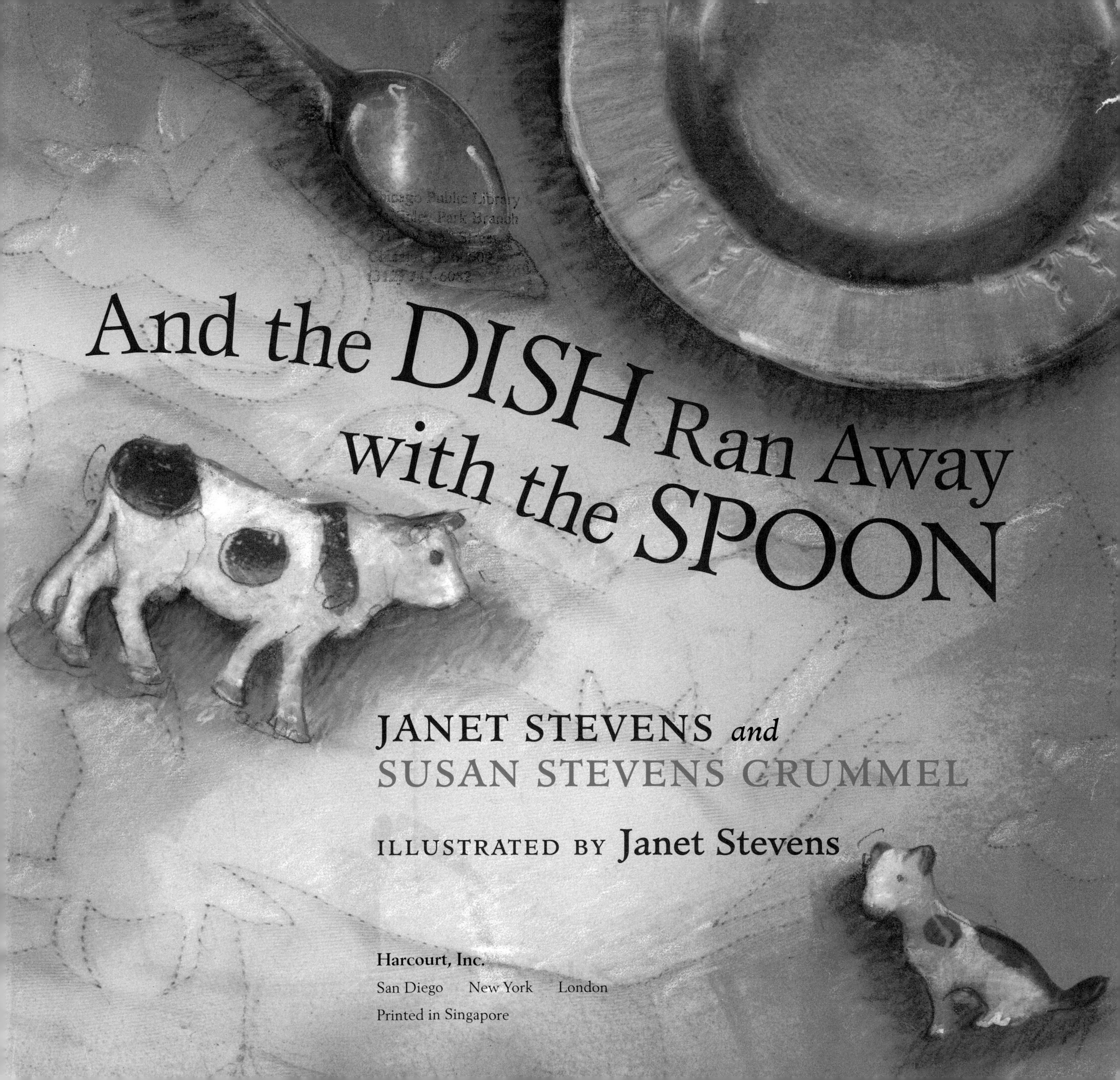

And the DISH Ran Away with the SPOON

JANET STEVENS and
SUSAN STEVENS CRUMMEL

ILLUSTRATED BY Janet Stevens

Harcourt, Inc.

San Diego   New York   London

Printed in Singapore

Hey diddle diddle, the cat and the fiddle,
The cow jumped over the moon;
The little dog laughed to see such sport,
And the dish ran away with the spoon.

"EVERYBODY UP!

They didn't come back!"

Cow opened one eye. "What do you mean, they didn't come back? Dish and Spoon *always* come back."

"Not this time!" said Cat. "Look, they're gone for good. History. Adiós."

"Leave 'em alone and they'll come home," mumbled Dog. "Now leave *me* alone. Can't you see I'm dog-tired?"

"*You're* tired?" said Cow. "Ever tried jumping over the moon?"

"Well, whoop-dee-doo to you," said Dog. "Why do we need Dish and Spoon anyway?"

"We just do," said Cat. "It's the way our rhyme goes. I fiddle, she jumps, you laugh, they run. Then they come back so we can do it again the next time! Without Dish and Spoon, there's no rhyme. No more diddle diddle. It's over."

"Why don't we just change their part?" Dog growled.

Cow yawned. "We could end it 'and the cow took a nap until noon.'"

"Or maybe 'and the little dog bit a baboon.'" Dog smirked.

"Stop fiddling around!" Cat demanded. "We don't have much time. You *know* our rhyme gets read every night, but it can't be read without Dish and Spoon. We have to find them *now*!"

Cow slowly got up. "Don't have a cow, Cat. I'm coming, I'm coming."

"Doggone it," muttered Dog. "I guess I'm coming, too."

So, off went the three with a hey diddle dee

by the light of the silvery moon—

to bring back the dish and the spoon.

the cat with his fiddle, the cow, and the dog.

Soon they came to a fork in the road.

"Excuse me, Fork, we're in a jam," said Cat. "Dish and Spoon ran away, and our rhyme can't be read without them. Can you help us?"

"Hmmm." Fork thought for a moment. "Let's see. A couple of lost sheep wandered by…Four-and-twenty blackbirds flew over…Oh yes, I remember seeing a dish…with little flowers on it…and a long, skinny spoon. In fact, they looked kind of familiar. I think we're from the same place setting!"

"Cut the blah, blah, blah and get to the point," said Dog. "Which way did they go?"

Fork glared. "You sure are a grumpy little dog. They could have gone any direction: north, south, east, west, northeast, northwest, westeast—"

"There's no westeast," interrupted Cat. "I'm confused. Maybe you could draw us a map."

"I'll take a stab at it," said Fork.

3 Men in a Tub

Wolf's House

Beanstalk

House that Jack Built

HUMPTY DUMPTY'S Wall

me

3 Bears' House

N
W ◆ E
S

mile

crooked mile

Garden
Water
meadow
dark forest
Not so dark forest

hill

path

Home

"Which way should we go?" asked Cat. "The Three Bears live one mile east and Little Boy Blue's haystack is one mile west."

"Three Bears," said Cow. "They say Mama Bear's bed is really soft."

Fork looked worried. "I wouldn't go there. The Bears don't like strangers dropping by."

"Then it's off to the haystack!" cried Cat.

With the blow of a horn and the cow in the corn,

the three headed off to the west—

the cranky ol' dog and the fiddlin' cat

and the cow who just wanted to rest.

"Here he is!" yelled Cat. "He's under this haystack, fast asleep."

"Wake up, lazy little boy!" barked Dog.

"*Shhh*. He looks so peaceful," whispered Cow. "I think I'll hit the hay, too."

"There's no time for a nap!" warned Cat. "Search this haystack!"

"Ah-h-h-h-h-h-choo-o-o-o-o-o-o-o!" Dog sneezed.

The haystack was gone.

"Well…no Dish and Spoon in there," said Cow.

Little Boy Blue rubbed his eyes. "Hey, where'd my haystack go?"

"Sorry, Dog has hay fever," Cat replied. "We're in a pickle. Dish and Spoon ran away, and our rhyme can't be read without them. Can you help us?"

"That's nothing to sneeze at." Little Boy Blue stretched. "But I've been asleep. I can't even find my cows and sheep. And where's that horn?"

"We're barking up the wrong tree," Dog grumbled. "Let's go north to Little Miss Muffet's."

With a curd and a whey and a dickory day,

and the dog with a scowl on her face.

they set out for Miss Muffet's place—

the cat with the fiddle, the cow who could jump,

Little Miss Muffet on.

Bo Peep

Wolf's House

House that Jack Built

School

3 Bears' House

me

N
W · E
S

Little Boy Blue

Home

A big, creepy spider sat on a tuffet. "May I help you?"

"We're in a mess," said Cat. "Dish and Spoon ran away—"

"Yeah," Spider interrupted. "I have the same problem with Muffet. I try to be nice, get to know her, even sit down beside her. Then *pffft!* Gone. Every time."

"But Muffet always comes back, right?" said Cow. "This time Dish and Spoon didn't come back. Are they here?"

"The only dishes here are the ones in the sink. Were your friends clean or dirty?" Spider asked.

"They were clean when they left," Dog said. "But who knows what they look like now."

Cat rummaged through the sink. "I don't see them. Now what?"

Spider grinned. "Why don't you try Wolf's house? It's about a mile east of here."

"You mean the *B-Big B-Bad Wolf*?" said Cow.

"He's not big and bad all the time," said Spider. "Why, Wolf is very kind to strangers. I bet he's having some for lunch right now!"

With a huff and a puff and a diddle dee duff,

by the hair of their chinny chin chins,

the cow and the dog and the cat traveled east

to where the dark forest begins.

"No bones about it," whispered Dog. "It's *dark* in this neck of the woods."

Cow stopped. "Why don't you two just go on ahead. I'll wait right here."

"Don't be a chicken," said Cat.

"I'm not a chicken, I'm a cow!"

"Then get a moooooove on," Cat ordered.

They crept deeper and deeper into the forest.

"Look," whispered Cat. "There's Wolf's house."

"I'm l-looking," Cow stammered. "It looks pretty big and bad to me."

Dog marched ahead. "Come on, I bet his bark is worse than his bite."

Wolf opened the door. "Hello, my little morsels. Come in and join me for lunch."

"We're in a predicament," said Cat bravely. "Dish and Spoon ran away, and our rhyme can't be read without them. Can you help us?"

"Of course I can." Wolf licked his chops. "But you three look so tired. I have a nice tub of hot water bubbling over the fire. First I can rub-a-dub-dub you down with a little seasoning. Uh, I mean bath oil."

Then Dog spotted it on the floor— a tiny chip of flowered china.

"Our friends!" she gasped. "What have you done with our friends?"

Wolf grabbed her. "Come on, you dirty dog, it's time to get in the tub. I'm just in the mood for a tasty dog treat."

"I'm not tasty," pleaded Dog. "I'm grumpy and tough!"

Wolf held Dog over the pot of boiling water. "Then you'll taste just like my mama's cooking!"

Cow screamed, "Let that little dog go!"

"But of course I'll let her go—right into the pot!" Wolf laughed. "Ha—ha—ha!"

Just then Cat had an idea. He put his fiddle under his chin and began to play a soft and tender lullaby.

Wolf stopped. He turned his head. "My mama . . . My mama . . . She used to sing that song to me every night before I went to sleep . . ."

Wolf cradled Dog in his arms and crooned, "Rock-a-bye, Wolfie, in your big bed . . ."

Wolf lay down on the floor. His big eyes closed and his big ears flopped. The Big Bad Wolf was fast asleep. Dog wriggled free. They all tiptoed past Wolf, then bolted out the door and down the path.

"Whew!" Cow sighed. "That was a close shave."

"We're not out of the woods yet," panted Dog.

Suddenly a voice boomed in the distance.

"Fee, fi, fo, fish, I smell the blood of a spoon and dish!"

Cat, Dog, and Cow froze.

"The voice is coming from the east," said Cow.

"It sounds like the giant!" cried Dog. "Dish and Spoon must be at the beanstalk."

Cat grabbed the map from Cow. "Oh no, the beanstalk! Look how far away it is!"

"I can help," said Cow. "Hop on. I'll get us there in a flash."

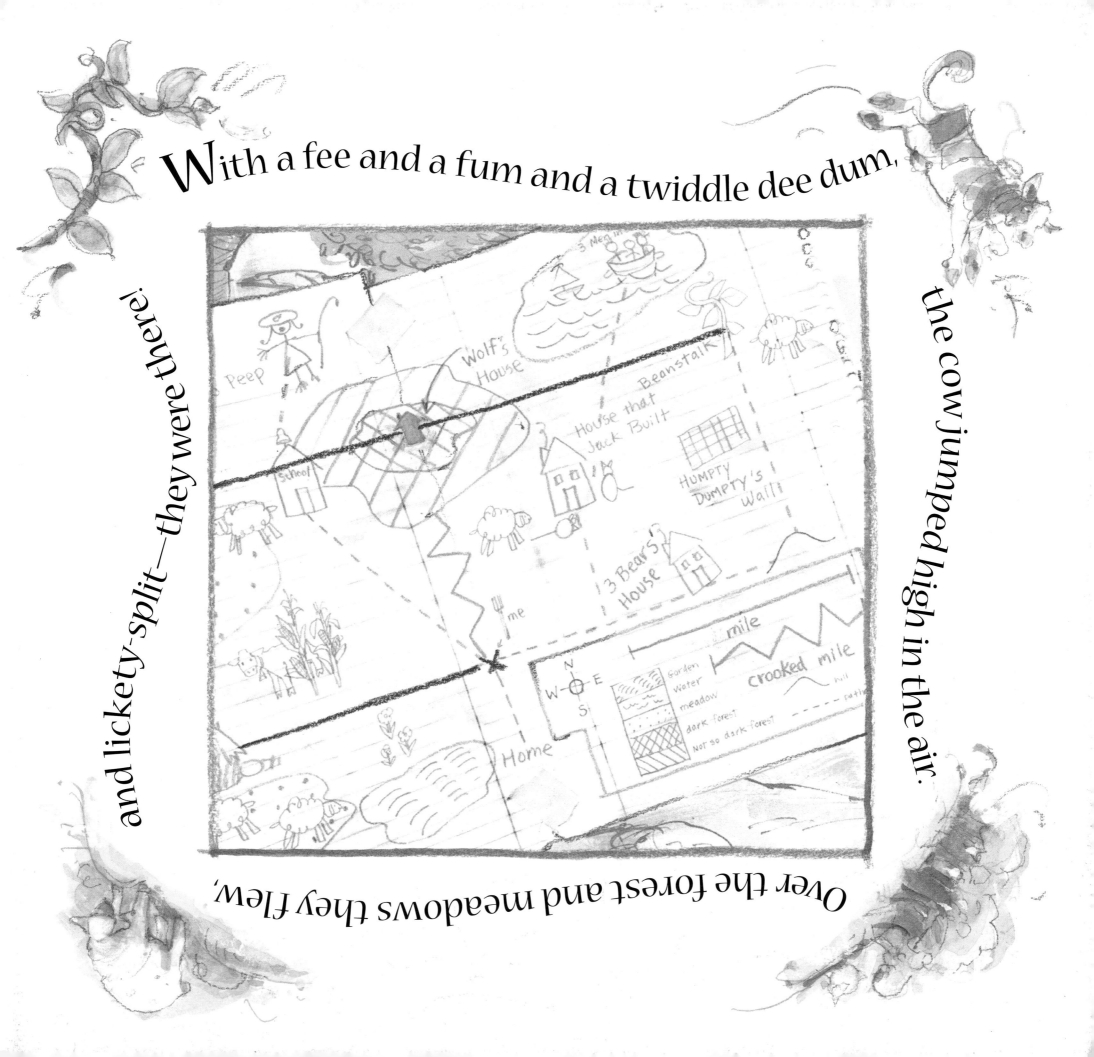

With a fee and a fum and a twiddle dee dum,
the cow jumped high in the air.
Over the forest and meadows they flew,
and lickety-split—they were there!

Cow, Cat, and Dog landed at the foot of the beanstalk.

"Hel-l-l-l-l-p!" came a cry from above. "We're falling down...falling down... falling dowwnnn—"

Crash!
BOING!

At last they had found Dish and Spoon.

Cat rushed over. "Spoon! Spoon! Are you all right?"

"I—I think so," said Spoon. "But—but—where's Dish?"

"She's over here," said Cow.

"And she's over here," said Dog.

"And she's over here, too," said Cat.

"Oh no!" cried Spoon. "She's everywhere!"

As they picked up the broken pieces, Spoon sobbed. "Wolf chased us up the beanstalk, then Giant chased us down the beanstalk and we slipped. We didn't mean to run away. Each time our rhyme was read, we went a little farther…and a little farther. This time we went *too* far and got lost. It was scary."

"Look—Dish is trying to say something," said Cow. "Quick. Put her mouth pieces together!"

"I want to go home," whispered Dish.

With Dish in a sack, they all headed back,

and hardly a sentence was spoken.

their friend and their hearts were broken.

The cat, the dog, the cow, and the spoon—

"Now what are we going to do?" Cat moaned as they traveled south toward home. "This is really the end. The final curtain. Dish is nothing but a pile of chips. Our rhyme is over forever!"

Dog stopped in her tracks. "Look, Humpty's wall. He falls apart every day. *Somebody* has to put him back together. Let's go find out *who*!" They raced toward the wall. Dog spotted a sign on a nearby tree:

JACK'S REPAIR SHOP
"You blew it, I glue it"

Inside Jack's shop, the floor was covered with eggshells, broken beds and chairs, snipped-off noses, and sticks and straw.

"What's the problem?" asked Jack, gluing a tail on a mouse.

"Dish went to pieces. Our rhyme has fallen apart. Can you help us?" Cat asked sadly.

"I *am* a jack-of-all-trades, and I'm nimble and quick, too!" Jack took the sack. "But this looks bad, really bad. I'll see what I can do."

They paced up and down with a fiddle dee frown—

Spoon, Little Dog, Cat, and Cow.

couldn't help anyone now!

All the king's horses and all the king's men

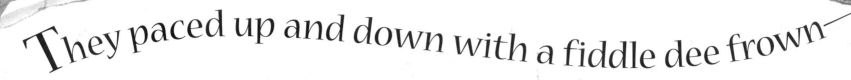

At last Jack returned—and Dish was right behind him.

"It was tough, but I stuck with it. See, Dish is as good as new!" said Jack. "Well, except for the missing piece."

"You mean this piece?" said Dog, holding out the chip of flowered china.

"You found it!" cried Dish. "It chipped off when I was running from Wolf. I crashed into that big pot!" Jack glued the chip in place.

"Hooray! Dish is back together and so are we!" Everyone cheered as they rushed outside.

Dish smiled at Dog. "I'm a full plate, thanks to you."

"When the chips are down, you can count on me." Dog chuckled. "Hey guys, did you hear that? I cracked a joke!"

Dish began to laugh—then Spoon—then Cow—then Cat. And then Dog threw her head back and laughed louder than anyone else.

"Who would've believed it?" said Cow. "Dog really laughed!"

"And Cat played the fiddle and saved us from Wolf," added Dog.

"And Cow got us to the beanstalk by jumping higher than ever!" said Cat. "Speaking of jumping, we'd better go—it's almost time!"

And in the winkin' blinkin'
of an eye, they were back home.

"Quick! Places, everyone!" yelled Cat.

Hey diddle diddle, the cat and the fiddle,
The cow jumped over the moon;
The little dog laughed to see such sport,
And the dish ~~ran away~~ stayed at home with the spoon.

For all the Jacks in our family: our grandfather, our dad, and
our brother (the real jack-of-all-trades)
                                                    —Love, Janet and Susie

Text copyright © 2001 by Janet Stevens and Susan Stevens Crummel
Illustrations copyright © 2001 by Janet Stevens

www.harcourt.com

Library of Congress Cataloging-in-Publication Data
Stevens, Janet.
And the dish ran away with the spoon/written by Janet Stevens and
Susan Stevens Crummel; illustrated by Janet Stevens.—1st ed.
p. cm.
Summary: When Dish and Spoon run away, their nursery rhyme friends
Cat, Cow, and Dog set out to rescue them in time for the next reading
of their rhyme.
[1. Characters in literature—Fiction.   2. Nursery rhymes—Fiction.]
I. Crummel, Susan Stevens.   II. Title.
PZ7.S84453An   2001
[E]—dc21   00-8861
ISBN 0-15-202298-8

First edition
H G F E D C B A

The illustrations in this book were done in watercolor, colored pencil,
and photographic and digital elements on watercolor paper.
The display type was set in Esprit and Minister.
The text type was set in Berling and Nueva MM.
Printed and bound by Tien Wah Press, Singapore.
This book was printed on totally chlorine-free Nymolla Matte Art paper.
Production supervision by Sandra Grebenar and Ginger Boyer
Designed by Lydia D'moch